Line drive.

But it was right at the second baseman.

Lian broke for second with the crack of the bat. But when he saw the catch, he braked and spun around.

He stumbled as he turned, however, and he was suddenly flat on his face.

The second baseman fired to first.

*"Ooooouuuutttt!"*

*Look for these books about the*
*Angel Park All-Stars*

# LINE DRIVE

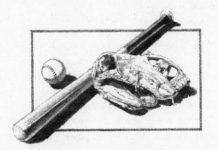

# By Dean Hughes
### Illustrated by Dennis Lyall

Bullseye Books • Alfred A. Knopf
New York

A BULLSEYE BOOK PUBLISHED BY ALFRED A. KNOPF, INC.
Copyright © 1990 by Dean Hughes
Cover art copyright © 1990 by Rick Ormond
Interior illustrations copyright © 1990 by Dennis Lyall
ANGEL PARK ALL-STARS characters copyright © 1989 by
Alfred A. Knopf, Inc.

Library of Congress Cataloging-in-Publication Data
Hughes, Dean, 1943–
Line drive / by Dean Hughes.
p. cm.—(Angel Park all-stars ; 7)
Summary: When Jeff Reinhold breaks his leg, a small
Asian boy named Lian Jie becomes the new second baseman.
ISBN 0-679-80432-3 (pbk.)—ISBN 0-679-90432-8 (lib. bdg.)
[1. Baseball—Fiction. 2. Asian Americans—Fiction.] I. Title.
II. Series: Hughes, Dean, 1943– Angel Park all-stars ; 7.
PZ7.H87312Li 1990
[Fic]—dc20 90-1609 CIP AC

RL: 4:7
First Bullseye Books edition: September 1990
Manufactured in the United States of America
1 2 3 4 5 6 7 8 9 10

*for Billy Nelson*

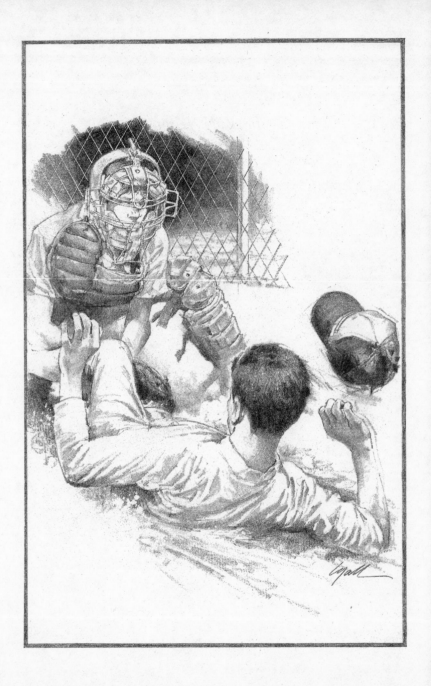

# ★ 1 ★

## Slide!

Harlan Sloan *leaped* for the ball. But he had no chance. It was hit like a rocket over his head and down the first-base line.

Jeff Reinhold, the runner on second, took off with the crack of the bat. Today was just a practice game, but Jeff played hard all the time.

Harlan spun around and looked at the right fielder as he snagged the ball. The kid was fast. He shot the ball to Danny Sandia at second base.

*"Home! Home!"* Harlan shouted to Danny. Jeff had rounded third and was racing toward the plate.

Danny spun and fired.

"*Slide!*" the third-base coach yelled.

Billy Bacon was blocking the plate, and he was waiting for the throw.

Jeff dropped into a slide. But he caught his ankle across Billy's shin.

Billy went flying, and the ball whizzed by.

Jeff was safe.

But he was in big trouble.

He let out a short, sharp scream. And then he rolled over on his side and grabbed at his leg.

"*Ooohhh. Oooohhhhhh. Oooooooohhhhhhh.*"

Harlan could hear the agony in Jeff's voice. He knew Jeff was badly hurt. Harlan ran toward the plate—and so did everyone else.

Coach Wilkens was one of the first to get there.

He kneeled down next to Jeff. "Where does it hurt?" he said.

Jeff tried to say something, but the words got lost in the groans.

Harlan couldn't believe it. How could this have happened in a practice game?

The coach had invited some of the guys from the Little League minors to come over, and they had divided up with the Dodgers to create a game situation for practice.

But now *this* had happened.

"Coach, I heard something pop," Billy said. He had his catcher's mask off now. The color was gone from his face.

"Everyone move back," the coach said.

But Sterling Malone was kneeling next to Jeff, and he didn't move.

"Sterling, you're good friends with Jeff," Coach Wilkens said. "Go call his parents, will you? Tell them to meet me at the emergency room, over at the hospital."

The coach bent close to Jeff. "Is it your ankle?" he asked.

"No. It's up here," Jeff gasped. He touched his shin. "I think it's broken."

Sterling had hesitated, but now he took off.

Harlan felt sort of sick. He backed away a little farther. Kenny Sandoval and Jacob Scott, Harlan's two best friends—and the other rookies on the team—came over to him.

"I wish he hadn't tried so hard to score," Kenny said. "It's only practice."

"He always plays hard. That's just the way he is," Jacob said.

Their voices were quiet.

The whole team was quiet.

They could see the pain in Jeff's face.

Rodney Bunson helped the coach carry Jeff to the car. The coach drove away, and then Bunson walked back to the others.

"I think it's bad," Bunson said. He was the Dodgers' star pitcher—a big kid, and usually loud. But his voice was soft now.

"He wanted to win the championship *so* bad," Jenny Roper said. She took off her hat and wiped the sweat from her forehead.

Henry White, the Dodgers' third baseman, asked the question that had suddenly struck Harlan. "Who'll play second base for us against the Giants?"

The players all knew what a big game that was. The Dodgers had won the season's first-half championship, but the Giants had lost only one game in the second half.

The Dodgers had lost two.

"Danny will," Bunson said, and he slapped his friend Danny Sandia on the back. "He'll do great."

Harlan wondered. Danny was the kind of player who would make a great play one time and muff the next one. And he lost his temper too easily. Players on other teams knew how to get him rattled.

Eddie Boschi, the skinny left fielder—and one of the Dodgers' pitchers—pointed at Harlan and Jacob. "I'll tell you one thing," he said. "You two guys will be playing more. You'll have to come through for us."

Harlan had already thought of that. But his stomach did a little flip-flop when he heard the words.

Bunson said, "What's the rule? Can't we

bring up another player from the minor league during the time Jeff can't play?"

"Yeah, I think so," Jenny said.

"We ought to get Cory," Bunson said. He pointed at a tall kid, one of the minor leaguers who had been playing with them today.

Cory was a sixth-grader, but he had never made the major league. Harlan thought he knew why. He was a decent player, but he was lazy—both in school and in baseball. Coach Wilkens didn't have a lot of patience with kids like that.

But Cory was also good friends with Bunson and Danny. They had wanted him on the team all along.

Bunson gave Cory a little punch on the shoulder, and Cory smiled, as though the whole thing were already settled.

"Maybe he's not hurt as bad as it looked," Henry said. "Maybe his leg is just bruised or something."

But Sterling shook his head. "No way,"

he said. "I was waiting on deck, so I heard it. Something really popped."

"I was just blocking the plate the way the coach always says to do," Billy said.

Harlan could see how bad he felt.

"Hey, it wasn't your fault," Henry said. "It just happened."

"Let's go down to the hospital," Brian Waters said. "Let's see what we can find out."

Everyone agreed.

And so the whole team walked across Angel Park, their little California desert town. They waited outside the hospital on the lawn. It was getting late in the afternoon now, but the air was still hot and dry.

Harlan sat with Jacob and Kenny and Brian. They talked about what they thought would happen if Jeff couldn't play.

"I'll tell you one thing," Brian said to Jacob. "It's no sure thing that Danny will play. The coach might put you in."

Jacob tried not to smile. He was a freckle-faced kid with a gap between his front teeth.

"I doubt it," he said. "He might even move Jenny to second base and let Harlan start at first."

"No, he wouldn't do that," Harlan said. "She's left-handed, and that doesn't work very well at second base." He stretched out on the grass. "Besides, I'm still the worst player on the team."

"You're a lot better than you were at the start of the season," Kenny said. "You've improved more than anyone."

"Do you really think so?" Harlan asked.

"Yup. I do."

Kenny did look serious. He nodded, and those dark eyes of his had that confident look—the way they did when he *knew* he was going to get a hit.

But Harlan wasn't sure. He didn't think the kids on the team believed in him. Kenny was a great player—a star. And Jacob had come through more often than Harlan had when the team really needed some help from the bench.

Harlan still felt like a rookie. Players teased him about his big ears, and they joked about his fielding at first base. They were a lot friendlier than they used to be, but they really didn't expect him to help the team very often.

"Here comes the coach," Kenny said.

Harlan sat up.

When he saw the coach's face, he already knew what he was going to say. But the words still sounded terrible.

"I'm afraid Jeff's leg is broken," Coach Wilkens said.

★ **2** ★

# Number Zero

When Wednesday came, Jeff showed up for the game.

But only to watch it.

He had a cast on his leg, and he was struggling along on crutches.

The coach had all the players sit on the grass just outside the four-diamond complex, where the Dodgers would be playing their big game.

"Kids," Coach Wilkens said, "I know you all feel bad about Jeff. And I do too. I wish I could say he'll be back to play before the season ends, but that just isn't going to happen."

"Coach?"

"Yeah, Sterling?"

Sterling was sitting near the front of the players, who were in a sort of half circle. "No one wanted to win the championship more than Jeff did," he said. "But now that he's not playing, we can't let it get us down."

All the players cheered. "Let's *kick* those Giants," Bunson yelled above the others.

The coach was nodding all this time. "That's great, kids. So let's do it."

Everyone cheered again, and some of the kids jumped up, but the coach said, "Wait a sec. There's one more thing."

Everyone sat down again.

"I'm going to bring up a player to replace Jeff. Some of you talked to me about Cory Stutz. The only trouble with that is, he's a sixth-grader. I thought it made more sense to use someone who could play with us next year."

Harlan watched Bunson and Danny. Their heads went down.

But the coach kept explaining. "A new kid moved to Angel Park not long ago. I've seen him play, and if he'd been around at the first of the season he would probably have made the team."

Harlan gulped. He was the last player the coach had chosen. This kid would have beaten him out. And that meant something else: the guy would probably get to play more than Harlan would.

"I've asked him to join us today," Coach Wilkens said, "but I had him wait in the bleachers until I explained the situation. Or at least I told him . . . as best as I could."

Harlan wondered what that meant.

The coach looked toward the bleachers and waved.

Everyone turned around to see who it was. But a little . . . *tiny* . . . boy was the only person coming out of the bleachers. He had to be a mascot or something.

The coach said, "I gave him Jeff's uniform, because that was the only one we had for now. But it doesn't fit very well."

Harlan couldn't believe his eyes. Didn't fit very well? Like Harlan wouldn't fit in one of his dad's suits!

The kid's pant legs were rolled up, and they still hung over his shoes. His short-sleeved shirt was a . . . long-sleeved shirt.

The boy turned around for a moment and looked back at his parents, who were yelling something to him. Was that Chinese?

"Zero?" Henry gasped.

Harlan knew what he meant. The number on the back of the kid's shirt was really a 9. But most of it was tucked down into his pants.

Usually the players let their shirts hang out—but this guy's shirt would have hung to his knees.

All the same, he had a baseball glove, and he was walking straight toward the Dodgers.

A few of the kids started to laugh.

Harlan just shook his head. This guy was going to go out there and play—looking like that? The Giants would laugh them out of the park.

"Players, I'd like you to meet . . . I'm sorry, but I can't say this very well. I think it's . . ."

The coach said something that Harlan couldn't quite get. It sounded something like "Leon Chi."

The new player bowed just a little. He had been smiling all along. He didn't seem nervous or embarrassed. In fact, he looked very pleased about something—maybe to be on the team.

"He only speaks a little English so far. He just moved here from Taiwan. But he played a lot of baseball over there. He's going to be a good one."

The players weren't saying a word. They were still staring at the kid.

He tugged at his sleeve and shrugged.

Then he said something that sounded like, "Fonny. Fonny."

"He means 'funny,' " Kenny finally said. "He knows the uniform looks weird on him."

"Does it ever," Danny mumbled.

But the coach jumped in. "All right, kids. Make him feel welcome. He understands more than he can say. He'll catch on quickly. He's a fourth-grader, so he'll be able to play for us two more years."

And then the coach added, "All right. Let's go out there and play our best."

And so the kids got up and went out to the field to warm up. But all the excitement about *kicking* the Giants had been lost for the moment.

Bunson and Danny were complaining, and the others were talking quietly.

The rookies were the ones who seemed to know the right thing to do. "This way," Harlan said. Then all three boys walked with the new boy onto the playing field.

He smiled at them and nodded—sort of

bowing again. Kenny asked, "What position do you play?"

The boy stared at him and shook his head.

"Po-si-tion," Kenny said again.

But Harlan knew what to do. He pointed to each of the bases and to the outfield positions. Then he shrugged his shoulders.

The boy nodded and smiled, and then he pointed to second and shortstop, and to center field.

"He plays the infield—second or short— or he can play center," Harlan said.

"Then he ought to warm up at second— where Jeff played," Jacob said.

Harlan knew that wasn't easy for Jacob. Jacob was wondering whether he might be starting at second today.

Harlan pointed to second, where Danny Sandia had already gone to take infield practice.

"After him," Harlan said, and he pointed to Danny and then to the boy. And he repeated the motion several times.

The Taiwanese boy nodded, seeming to understand, and then he ran toward Danny. He kept going, beyond Danny, and he stopped and waited.

"Yes," Harlan yelled. "Yes." And then to Danny, "Let him take a turn in a few minutes."

Danny didn't answer, but Harlan could see he didn't like the idea.

All the same, after Danny had taken a few ground balls, the coach yelled out. "Okay, now let . . . uh . . . Leon—or whatever it is—take a few."

Danny moved back. The boy moved up.

Coach Wilkens hit a ground ball, rather sharply, toward the new boy. He moved in for it just right, but at the last second he stumbled. He tried to catch himself and field the ball, but he tumbled forward and the ball hit him and bounced away.

He didn't get up.

Harlan ran to him.

But by then the boy had begun to stir. As

he got up he was rubbing his neck. The ball had made a big red mark.

"Are you okay?" Harlan asked.

"Okay," the kid said. He nodded and smiled. But Harlan could tell he was still in pain.

All the same, he motioned for the coach to go ahead, and he got ready for another grounder.

But now the Giants were starting to show up. They didn't say anything when it looked like the boy might be hurt, but as soon as they saw he was all right, they started in.

Cranny Crandall—the smart-mouthed catcher—started the insults.

"Hey, Dodgers, you gotta be kidding," he yelled. "Is that little kid wearing his pajamas?"

Harlan was just glad that Leon—or whatever his name was—couldn't understand.

But he had to admit, the poor kid *did* look like he was wearing pajamas.

# ★ 3 ★

# Giant Trouble

The Giants couldn't have been happier.

The new kid kept stumbling around, his big uniform flopping in the breeze. He couldn't seem to stop a ground ball or throw it—or anything else.

He kept pulling at his uniform, trying to straighten it out. Harlan felt sorry for him. He knew the poor guy didn't have a chance. The pant legs kept catching his heels, and the sleeves got in the way of his throwing motion.

He was pretty sure that the boy had good skills. He couldn't be as bad as he looked right now, or the coach wouldn't have chosen him.

After the boy took a few grounders, he stepped back to let Danny have another turn. He looked at Harlan and tugged on his uniform again. "Big," he said. "Too big."

Harlan nodded and smiled. "Leon" smiled too. Harlan was amazed at what a good sport he was.

Harlan walked over to him. "Tell me how to say your name," he said.

"Name?"

"Yes."

"Lee-en Ji," was what Harlan thought he heard. But the boy dropped to one knee and wrote in the dirt L-I-A-N J-I-E. Then he spoke the name again. "Lian Jie."

"Lee-en Ji," Harlan said.

The boy nodded. "Yes." He pointed at Harlan. "Name?"

"My name is Harlan."

That was difficult for Lian. "Harran," he said.

Both boys laughed. "Close enough," Harlan said.

But just then "Heat" Halliday, the Giants' star pitcher, yelled, "Hey, kid, the T-ball games aren't till tomorrow."

And Cranny was at it again. "Don't get lost inside that uniform, little guy. We'd hate to have to send in a search party to look for you."

Lian didn't understand the words. Still, he must have known they were making fun of him. But he kept smiling. Harlan had the feeling he knew what he could do and wasn't worried—except about the uniform.

It was the rest of the team that seemed down. They had come out ready to win one for Jeff, but now they had lost something. Harlan knew that the players were embarrassed about Lian.

All the same, Sterling looked up at Jeff in the bleachers behind the dugout. "We're going to win this one for you," he yelled.

Jeff grinned and held up his clenched fist. He was sitting with his parents. He had his leg propped up in front of him.

When the team gathered in the dugout, and Henry walked out to face Halliday, Jenny said, "All right, now, let's forget everything but this game. This is one we gotta win."

Some of the spirit seemed to come back. After all, Lian was on the bench. The Giants had forgotten him for now. The Dodgers knew they had to win, and that was enough to fire them up.

It just wasn't enough to cool the heat— Heat Halliday, that is.

Henry tried to get something started with a surprise bunt, but the ball rolled foul. Heat blazed the next two pitches past him. Henry rarely struck out. But he did this time.

Cranny loved it. "That's the first of eighteen," he shouted. "Heat promised me a perfect game today."

That sort of stuff only made the Dodgers angry. Sterling stepped into the box. He said something that Harlan couldn't hear—and then Cranny's mouth starting moving.

"I can smell rotten potatoes clear over here," Billy Bacon said. "Cranny doesn't just *look* like a bag of potatoes. I think he *is* a bag of potatoes."

But Sterling, no matter what he told Cranny, swung and missed a smoking fastball. Cranny laughed and Sterling swung harder the next time, but he lifted an easy fly into center field.

Two outs.

"Two down and sixteen to go," Cranny yelled. "And the little rookie coming up."

Kenny didn't seem to be bothered. And he did have a good swing. But he grounded the ball to second base, and that was all for the Dodgers.

"Only five innings to go," Cranny yelled to the Dodgers. "This one's a piece of cake."

But the umpire grabbed Crandall's shoulder as he was about to run away. Harlan knew that the ump was telling Cranny that enough was enough.

What worried Harlan was that the team

had had trouble before when they let themselves get upset. He also knew that Heat had his good stuff going, and he was going to be tough, no matter what.

But Bunson, the kid everyone in the league now called "Burner," could be just as tough.

He showed it in the first inning.

He did give up a walk to Dave Weight, the tough-hitting third baseman.

But then he got the cleanup hitter to pop up and end the inning.

Cranny didn't mouth off as much in the second inning, but he kept counting the outs. When Bunson flied out, he held up four fingers, and when Jenny bounced out, he held up five.

"What's he going to do next, catch without a glove—just so he'll have enough fingers to show us?" Billy said.

"No," Sterling said. "Because Brian's going to get a hit and stop this stupid show."

But Brian was overmatched against Heat

today. He tried to work him for a walk, and then, in desperation, tried to bunt with two strikes. But he fouled the ball off and was out.

Back to the field.

Cranny waited until he was well away from the umpire and then yelled, "Six down, twelve to go. *Noooooo problem.*"

At that point his own coach told him to shut his mouth, but Cranny only laughed, and when his coach wasn't looking, he held up six fingers for all the Dodgers to look at.

It was maddening.

Harlan sat next to Lian. He wondered how much he understood of all this.

"No hits, Lee-en," Harlan said, shaking his head.

Lian nodded. He made a swinging motion, and then with the other hand, showed the ball going by—fast.

"Good pitchers," Harlan said.

"Yes. Very good."

"Good pitchers in Taiwan?"

"Yes. Very good."

Halliday was stepping up to bat.

"Good batter, too," Harlan said. He pointed to Halliday, and then made a swinging motion.

"Good batter," Lian said.

Harlan was starting to wonder whether he understood or was only repeating.

But then Halliday stung the ball on the ground toward second.

Danny stepped back and let the ball bounce hard toward his shins. He reached down, but the ball got under his glove. It glanced off Danny's leg and rolled into right field.

"Oh, no," Harlan said.

"Bad," Lian said. "Very bad."

Harlan looked at him, and the boy stood up and made an imitation of Danny's technique. He stepped back and pushed his glove down, straight-armed. "Very bad," he said again.

And then he stepped forward and crouched, low, with his left leg forward. It was exactly what the coach taught the players to do.

"You *do* know baseball," Harlan said.

But Lian didn't seem to understand.

Harlan was trying to think how to explain when he heard a sickening *crack*.

The first baseman, a big kid named Glenn, had just hammered a Bunson fastball. Harlan looked up to see the ball turning into a little white pill in a blue, blue evening sky.

"That ball may end up in Los Angeles," Harlan said.

Lian didn't understand, but he knew the problem.

"Very bad," he said.

And now it was Harlan's turn to repeat the words. "Very bad," he said. "Very, *very* bad."

# ★ 4 ★

# Disappearing Act

---

Harlan was worried. So often, once Bunson got upset, he pitched worse.

But not today.

He settled down and got the next two batters on soft grounders. When Crandall came up, Bunson put something extra on the ball, but he didn't mess up his motion.

He made Cranny look stupid. The guy took two bad swings, and then tried for a walk. He let a couple of close ones go by.

He complained like crazy when he got called out on strikes.

"That's what you do best with that big mouth," Bunson yelled to him. "Cry like a baby."

But Coach Wilkens didn't like that. He yelled to Bunson, "Don't get that stuff started."

"*He* started it," Bunson said.

"Then you stop it," the coach answered.

Harlan saw Bunson roll his eyes. That sort of thing was hard for Bunson. But he was doing a lot better than he had early in the season.

Cranny got his catcher's gear on. When he walked from the dugout, he yelled, "Okay, send on the seventh out. Oh, good, it's you, Danny. You're the easiest out in the lineup."

Danny had a few things to say, but nothing loud enough for the coach to hear. And then he swung as if he were trying to put the ball into orbit—but he didn't touch it.

Two more swings and he was out. He threw his bat at the fence as he stalked away from the plate.

Coach Wilkens yelled, loud enough for everyone to hear, "Jacob, go in for Danny when we go back to the field."

Danny walked into the dugout and tossed his glove. But he kept his mouth shut.

Harlan really hated to see this kind of stuff happening.

But the frustration kept growing.

Eddie Boschi also struck out.

Billy Bacon rolled a little grounder out in front of the plate. Cranny jumped on it and threw him out, and then he spun around and said, "Hey, Bacon Burger, we're halfway there."

It was all Billy could do to walk away without saying anything. Harlan could see that.

Harlan was still in the dugout. He hoped he would get in the game soon. He looked around when he heard Jeff yell, "Come on, you guys. You can do it."

Harlan waved to him, and then shouted, "Come on, team. We gotta do this for Jeff."

And Bunson put away the Giants, one, two, three.

But Heat knocked over the Dodgers the same way.

That was trouble. White, Malone, and Sandoval were the guys who usually came through. Now there were only six outs to go. The way Halliday was throwing, those guys might not come up again.

And Cranny was loving every second of it.

He ran toward the dugout and then stopped. He drew a line in the dirt. Then he drew another and another, and Harlan saw what was coming. When he had drawn the last one, he spun around and said, "That's *twelve dead Dodgers* marked off. *Just six* to go."

Harlan looked over at Lian, who was shaking his head again. "Very bad," he was muttering. "Very bad."

"Harlan, go in at first," Coach Wilkens yelled. "Tell Lian"—he pronounced it "Leon"—"to play second." Then he looked at Jacob. "Move to right field."

Harlan grabbed Lian's arm and led him out of the dugout, and he pointed toward second base. Lian nodded, and then ran to his position.

When he got there, he looked over at Harlan. His little smile was still there.

But Harlan was worried. With Jenny and Brian out of the lineup, those last six outs would be easier to get. He and Lian were surely not as tough with the bat as they were.

And what if Lian had trouble playing second, the way he did in warm-ups?

The Giants were thinking the same way. The laughter poured out of the dugout when they saw Lian take the field.

"Hit the ball to the right side," Halliday yelled to the batter stepping in. "With that midget playing second, and Dumbo the elephant playing first, *everything* will get through."

The umpire told the Giants to quiet down again, but Harlan had already felt the sting. Those guys always joked about his big ears.

At least there was one thing the Giants weren't joking about—the Dodgers' fielding. They *did* try to hit the ball to the right side. But the cleanup hitter got under the ball, and Jacob made the catch in the outfield.

Halliday then chopped a ground ball right at Harlan. Harlan took a high hop and ran to the bag.

He took a little pleasure in looking Halliday in the eye as he had to turn and trot back to his dugout.

But then the Giants' first baseman hit a grounder toward Lian.

Harlan waited for the throw. He saw Lian stride forward just right, and he watched him get down, ready to field the ball.

But his pant leg caught his foot again, and he was thrown off balance. The ball took a flat hop and . . . disappeared.

Lian spun around, but the ball was gone. He glanced up at Harlan as if to say, "What happened?"

Harlan was as baffled as Lian.

The runner had rounded first and was

heading for second, but he was looking around for the ball too.

And then Lian grabbed at his side.

Harlan thought he was hurt.

Suddenly Lian yanked his shirttail out— and the ball plopped on the ground!

The runner was heading for third.

Lian grabbed the ball and made a decent throw to third, but it was too late. The runner slid in ahead of the tag.

Harlan had finally realized what had happened. The ball had gone right up Lian's baggy sleeve and into his shirt.

Harlan could see how embarrassed Lian was. He tugged at the shirt again and shook his head.

The Giants, meanwhile, were losing it. They were falling all over one another, laughing as though they would die.

Bunson didn't think it was quite so funny.

He stared at Lian for a time, and then glanced over at Harlan and shook his head.

"Wait a second," Harlan said to Bunson,

and then he spun and called to the umpire, "Time-out."

Harlan hurried over to Lian. "Let's see what we can do with this thing," he said. He stepped behind Lian and pulled the uniform into a lump in the back. That did draw the shirt together, but Harlan needed some way to keep it that way. "Does someone have a safety pin?" he shouted to the crowd.

The Giants' players laughed again, and one of them yelled, "Why a pin? Does he need his diaper changed?"

All the same, a woman came forward with a pin—actually a couple of them—and she even helped Harlan pin up the back of the uniform and roll up the sleeves a little better.

Lian didn't look much better, but it was the best they could do for the moment.

Bunson was disgusted with the whole mess. He let fly with a pitch that was way over Billy Bacon's head. The run scored from third on the wild pitch.

This brought on lots more shouts and taunts from the Giants.

But at least Bunson made a good second pitch, and the batter hit a come-backer to Bunson. He ran the ball to first rather than take a chance throwing, and then he said to Harlan, "That little kid's going to ruin us."

"He's not really that bad, I don't think," Harlan said. "It's that uniform that's causing his problems."

"Yeah, right," Bunson said.

Bunson was next up to bat, and he was mad. As he got a bat from the rack he told the players who were walking into the dugout, "Okay, the no-hitter ends now."

But it didn't. Bunson did hit the ball hard, but he hit it to straightaway center. Dodero, the fast center fielder, ran hard and caught up with it.

Harlan was now up, and Lian was on deck. No wonder Bunson had been so sure he had to be the one to break up the no-hitter.

Harlan told himself he wouldn't listen to

Cranny and the other Giants. But Cranny started right off with, "Fifteen down and three to go."

It took a couple of seconds for that to sink in, and then Harlan looked at Cranny curiously.

"Oh, I've already counted you and the little midget over there. You'll never get a hit off Heat. He remembers that you got a hit off him once before. He's *waiting* for you."

Harlan looked out at Halliday. He was glaring in at Harlan. And his first pitch was like a cannon shot. Harlan was not even sure that he saw it.

But he knew he couldn't hit the ball if he didn't swing. He also knew that Heat was too sharp today to walk him.

And so, on the next pitch, he swung as the ball left Heat's hand. No one in the park was more surprised than Harlan when he felt the bat connect. The ball shot over the second baseman's outstretched glove and into right field.

Harlan took off for first base. When he got there, he was still not sure he believed it.

The Dodgers were all cheering for Harlan, and Bunson yelled, "Hey, Cranny, now you can start counting all the base hits."

Heat was mad enough to eat the baseball when he got it back. Poor little Lian was going to face one very mad Giant.

# ★ 5 ★

# Blooper

Lian had a good stance—except for all the extra uniform hanging off him. Harlan was pretty sure the little guy knew how to handle a bat.

He could also see that Heat wanted to *burn* him.

But his first pitch was high. Lian didn't leave much of a strike zone to shoot at.

Cranny had stopped talking about no-hitters.

He sounded almost angry when he yelled, "Come on, Heat. Bring it down. No way this kid can hit it."

Heat brought it down some, and he took a little off his fastball, but the ball was still up in Lian's eyes.

Lian didn't swing. He glanced down at Harlan and nodded, as though he knew what was coming next.

Heat took a lot off his pitch and aimed it lower this time.

Lian swung. He hit a little blooper that flared off to the right. It was just over the first baseman's head and . . . barely inside the line.

A *base hit!*

The second baseman caught up with the ball in foul territory. Harlan rounded second and ran hard to third. The throw was to third, and it was close, but Harlan slid in safe.

Lian held at first.

He stood on the bag, with his hands on his hips—a strange picture. His sleeves were down to his wrists and flopping in the breeze, and his shirt was pulled up so it bloused out around the middle.

But he didn't seem at all surprised to be at first base. He had that little smile on his face, and he looked very calm.

No one else in the park could *believe* he was standing there!

He hadn't hit the ball hard. He had only dropped it in a perfect spot. Just the same, he had done what all the big guns for the Dodgers hadn't been able to do.

"You got lucky," Heat yelled. He kicked at the dirt on the mound.

All the other Giants were yelling the same kind of stuff.

The Dodgers were getting psyched. Jacob was the batter—not one of those big guns either—but the way things were going, maybe he was their best shot.

And maybe Heat was losing it.

But he soon put that idea to rest.

*Bam!*

He fired a fastball that sent dust flying from Cranny's mitt.

Jacob stepped away and took a deep breath.

"Come on, Jacob," Harlan was yelling. "Bring me home."

And Jacob did give it a shot. He swung at the next pitch and tagged it.

Line drive.

But it was right at the second baseman.

Lian broke for second with the crack of the bat. But when he saw the catch, he braked and spun around.

He stumbled as he turned, however, and he was suddenly flat on his face.

The second baseman fired to first.

*"Ooooouuuutttt!"*

Double play.

The rally was suddenly over.

The Giants were celebrating, and the Dodgers were saying they would get them next inning.

But it didn't happen. White did get another hit off Heat in the last inning, but that was all the Dodgers could get going.

For the first time all season the Dodgers had been shut out.

Worse than that, for the second time in a row, the Dodgers had lost to the Giants.

And worst of all, they hadn't come through for Jeff.

Harlan looked up at him. He nodded as if to say, "You gave it your best shot," but Harlan felt rotten.

That would have been bad enough without having to listen to Cranny and Heat—and all the rest of the Giants. "You can forget about winning the second half," Heat yelled. "You guys just *went down the drain.*"

After the game, the coach gave one of his talks about baseball being fun even when the team lost. He said the players had to learn to lose and not let it get them down.

But as Harlan walked home with Jacob

and Kenny that night, he found out that he wasn't the only one who had a hard time accepting that.

"I thought we had the championship for sure after we won all our games in the first half," Kenny said.

"The Giants are six and one for the second half," Jacob said. "And we're four and three. Tonight the Reds will probably beat the Mariners, and they'll be five and two."

"I never thought we'd be in *third* place," Harlan said.

All three walked in silence for a time.

Finally Harlan said, "We still won the first half, so we'll be in the play-off for the championship no matter what happens."

"Yeah. Against the Giants," Jacob said.

Harlan heard his discouragement.

But Kenny said, "The Reds and the Giants could still lose some games. We always play against their best pitchers. They aren't so hot when they use their other guys."

That was true.

But Harlan was thinking about one more thing.

And wondering.

"I wish we'd had Jeff today," Kenny said. "I'm not so sure that Lian kid is going to be very good."

"I don't know if we can beat *anyone* with him playing," Jacob said.

So they were all wondering the same thing.

But Harlan had a feeling Lian could play. "I don't think that hit Lian got was just an accident," he said. "He had a good swing. And he knows how to make contact."

"I hope you're right," Kenny said. But he didn't sound convinced.

If Kenny was doubtful, most of the guys on the team were downright depressed—or mad—about Lian.

At practice on Thursday night Lian still

had on that huge uniform. His mother had pinned it up better, but it was still a mess. The coach said he had ordered a new one, and it would be coming in a week or two.

A week or two?

Harlan couldn't believe it. He was almost sure that Lian's trouble was that he couldn't move right in all that extra cloth.

But when Harlan said that to some of the players, Bunson said, "No way, Harlan. That kid can't play—no matter what he has on."

Danny agreed, of course.

At the moment, Harlan was waiting his turn during batting practice. Some of the other players were waiting too. Little Lian was out in the field taking grounders.

And he didn't look that bad.

But just then Lian let a grounder get by him, and Sterling said, "He may not be as bad as he looks, but, man—he looks *real bad*. There is no way that he'll ever be as good as Jeff."

Harlan wasn't sure why he felt he was the

guy who had to defend Lian, but he said, "Hey, he got a hit didn't he? Halliday was getting everyone out, and he got a hit."

"So did you," Danny said. "Anyone can luck out."

Bunson laughed.

Just then the coach yelled, "Leon . . . er . . . tell me how to say your name again."

Lian yelled his name. "Lee-en Ji," he pronounced it.

The coach yelled back, "Line Ji?"

Lian nodded and smiled as if to say, "That's close enough."

But Bunson said, "Did you hear that? The kid's name is Line Drive. No wonder he got that great hit in the game."

"Yeah, it was a long fly," Danny said. "Clear out of the infield."

Bunson laughed. "Hey, that's where he got his name. He hits those 'line Ji's' all the time."

"Come on, you guys," Harlan said. "Give the guy a chance."

"A chance? Heck, he's our star," Bunson said. "What other team has a player named Line Drive? When pitchers hear his name, they'll be shaking in their boots."

# BOX SCORE, GAME 17

## Angel Park Dodgers 0          Blue Springs Giants 3

| | ab | r | h | rbi | | ab | r | h | rbi |
|---|---|---|---|---|---|---|---|---|---|
| White 3b | 3 | 0 | 1 | 0 | Nugent lf | 2 | 0 | 0 | 0 |
| Malone cf | 3 | 0 | 0 | 0 | Sanchez ss | 2 | 0 | 0 | 0 |
| Sandoval ss | 2 | 0 | 0 | 0 | Weight 3b | 1 | 0 | 0 | 0 |
| Bunson p | 2 | 0 | 0 | 0 | Dodero cf | 2 | 0 | 0 | 0 |
| Roper 1b | 1 | 0 | 0 | 0 | Halliday p | 2 | 1 | 1 | 0 |
| Waters rf | 1 | 0 | 0 | 0 | Glenn 1b | 2 | 2 | 2 | 2 |
| Sandia 2b | 1 | 0 | 0 | 0 | Zonn rf | 1 | 0 | 0 | 0 |
| Boschi lf | 2 | 0 | 0 | 0 | Cooper 2b | 1 | 0 | 0 | 0 |
| Bacon c | 2 | 0 | 0 | 0 | Crandall c | 2 | 0 | 0 | 0 |
| Scott rf | 1 | 0 | 0 | 0 | Villareal lf | 1 | 0 | 0 | 0 |
| Sloan 1b | 1 | 0 | 1 | 0 | Hausberg rf | 1 | 0 | 0 | 0 |
| Jie 2b | 1 | 0 | 1 | 0 | Spinner ss | 1 | 0 | 0 | 0 |
| ttl | 20 | 0 | 3 | 0 | | 18 | 3 | 3 | 2 |

**Dodgers**  0  0  0  0  0  0—0
**Giants**  0  2  0  1  0  x—3

# Perfect Fit

When Harlan got to the park on Saturday morning, there was Lian by one of the diamonds. He was in his street clothes except for his Dodgers' baseball cap, and he was talking to the coach, who looked very confused.

As Harlan came closer he heard Lian say, "No play? No play?"

But the coach was nodding, saying, "Yes, you *do* play."

Harlan had the feeling, from the way Coach Wilkens was emphasizing his words, that he had said them a few times before.

"What's going on?" Harlan asked.

"I wish I knew," the coach said. "He showed up without his uniform, and he keeps asking me if he's going to play."

Harlan suddenly understood.

"I have it," Harlan said to Lian. He held out the folded uniform.

Lian looked happy as he took the uniform and nodded, but Harlan could tell he was still confused.

"My mother fixed it," he said. "So it will fit you better."

Lian was staring.

"Uh, let's see," Harlan said, holding the uniform up to him. "Fits better now." Harlan showed him one of the sleeves his mother had hemmed up. Then he pointed to the men's room beyond the diamond. "Put it on."

Lian understood. He nodded several times, and then he took off for the men's room.

"I still don't understand what's going on," the coach said.

"I went over to his house last night and got his uniform," Harlan said. "I tried to explain why I wanted it, but I guess he didn't understand. He must have thought he was kicked off the team."

The coach laughed. "No wonder he was so upset. But that was a good idea, Harlan—to fix his uniform."

"It was really my mom's idea. She shortened the sleeves and the legs, and she tightened everything up. She's good at stuff like that."

"Well, tell her thanks," Coach Wilkens said.

But neither he nor Harlan was quite ready for what they saw when Lian came back. His shirt was still tucked deep into his pants, but the uniform looked good—and Lian looked overjoyed.

That was not what surprised everyone, though.

Lian was a whole new kid. Now that he could move the way he needed to—and maybe felt a boost to his confidence—he started eating up grounders like a natural. Nothing was getting by him.

"Look at that," Billy said, as Lian made a perfect throw to Jenny at first base. "He's got a good arm for a guy that size."

"I know," Sterling said. "He just back-handed a ball that Jeff would have missed. He's *fast*."

The A's were noticing too. Some of them had stopped their warm-ups and were watching Lian. "Who *is* that kid?" Harlan heard them asking.

But Bunson had his doubts. "Old Line Drive doesn't look too bad," he said, and he laughed. "But the bat's bigger than he is. He's probably already had the only hit he'll ever get."

When the game started, Kenny was on the mound. Lian was on the bench with Harlan and Jacob. So it would be a while before the team found out what Lian could do.

Kenny looked determined. The Dodgers *had* to win today.

"This is a *very* big game for the Dodgers," Jacob announced in his radio voice. "They have their backs to the wall."

"Yeah, Frank, that's right," he said in his cowboy voice. "But then, that's better than having their fronts to the wall. It ain't easy to see anything in that position."

Kenny delivered his first pitch, a thumping fastball.

Strike one.

Harlan turned to Jacob and said, "I hope the Reds can beat the Giants today. They play right after us."

Swing and a miss. Strike two.

"I wish they could *both* lose," Jacob said.

"Yeah, me too. But I thought the Reds would beat the Mariners Wednesday night, and they didn't. So they got three losses, the same as us. Now we need the Giants to lose one."

"Hey, batta, batta, batta," the infield was yelling.

*Pop.*

Strike three.

Kenny was looking *tough.*

All the Dodgers cheered, and they yelled to Kenny to go after the next guy.

"Right now we gotta beat the A's and not worry about what the rest of them do," Jacob said.

That was right. And Kenny looked as if he could take care of things. He let loose with an off-speed pitch that the batter backed away from. But it broke over the plate for strike one.

"Curb ball," Lian said.

"That's right. Curve ball," Harlan said. He and Jacob grinned.

During the next couple of innings, Harlan found out that Lian knew *plenty* about baseball.

When the Dodgers came up to bat, Lian watched closely as White opened with a single. When Malone hit the ball down the right field line, the right fielder ran after it and then spun and threw as hard as he could.

But he tried to throw all the way to third, and his arm wasn't strong enough. The ball was over the relay man's head but nowhere near third. By the time the shortstop ran the ball down, Henry had scored.

"Not good," Lian said. He pointed to the second baseman. "Throw to him," he said, although he struggled to pronounce the words.

"That's right," Harlan said. "He's the cut-off man."

That was the kind of stuff Harlan had learned from Coach Wilkens, but not everyone in Little League was taught so well.

"Lian knows his baseball," Jacob said.

"Yes," Lian said. He laughed and nodded.

Harlan laughed too. He liked this kid.

Things kept getting better. Kenny hit a line-drive single, and Malone scored. And after Bunson walked, Jenny drove home Kenny on a misjudged fly ball that should have been caught by the center fielder.

After a couple of outs, Brian Waters came through with another single, bringing home Bunson.

And so, when the first inning was over, the Dodgers had themselves a 4 to 0 lead.

With Kenny looking good on the mound, the game seemed in control.

But then the Reds and the Giants, who were playing against each other in the next game, started to show up. Both teams, and all their fans, began to cheer for the A's.

The Dodgers had expected that, and they didn't pay much attention. But it wasn't long before the razzing started, as usual, and some of it wasn't very funny.

When Danny Sandia came up to bat in the second inning, the Reds' players tried to get to him. "Don't get mad, Danny," one of them yelled. "You know what happens when you lose your temper."

When he swung at the first pitch and missed, Harlan heard that booming voice of Winter, the Reds' huge catcher. "Oh, *no,* Danny, you're losing your temper."

Everyone got in on the act. "Don't get mad, Danny," someone yelled again, and then it turned into a chant.

"Don't get *mad,* Danny. Don't get *mad,* Danny."

But Danny did. He struck out on a pitch that was in the dirt. And then he threw his bat down and yelled to the kids in the stands to shut up.

Harlan could see trouble ahead.

# ★ 7 ★

# Tough Call

---

"Everyone, listen to me," Coach Wilkens said.

The team was about to go back out on the field to start the third inning.

"You can't let those kids get to you. We've been through this kind of stuff before. Just play ball."

"They're just trying to make us mad," Sterling said.

"It *won't work* this time," Brian yelled.

"That's right," some of the players yelled, and then the team ran back to the field.

But the coach grabbed Danny. Harlan heard him say, "Danny, don't let us down. Those kids will keep working on you if they think you're listening."

"Okay," Danny said. He nodded firmly.

Jacob and Harlan and Lian were all standing in the dugout. They knew this was a crucial time in the game. Or at least Harlan thought that Lian understood what was happening.

The second baseman, eighth in the lineup, was coming up. He wasn't much of a hitter.

Kenny's first pitch was outside, but then he brought in a fastball at the knees that left the kid standing there.

But on the next pitch the kid punched at the ball and sent a weak grounder to the right side. Danny charged, grabbed it nicely, and spun and flipped the ball to Jenny. But the throw was wide, and Jenny had to stretch for it.

The infield umpire threw up his thumb and barked, *"Out!"*

At the same instant the plate umpire yelled, *"Safe!"*

What?

"The runner is safe," the plate umpire

yelled. "The first baseman pulled her foot off the bag."

Both of the umpires were young guys, maybe high school ballplayers. Harlan wondered whether they were that well trained.

Danny wondered, too, but he wondered out loud. "What? What are you talking about?" he yelled.

Coach Wilkens hurried toward home plate. He didn't raise his voice, but Harlan heard him say, "Umpire, that's *his* call." He pointed toward the other umpire. "He called the boy out."

"I know. But I'm the head umpire, so I can overrule him. And I saw the player's foot come off the bag."

"And you're sure you could see better than the other ump—even from this distance?"

The young man nodded. "Her foot came off the bag."

"All right," Coach Wilkens said, and he turned to go back to the third-base coach's box.

But Danny was still upset. "No way," he yelled. "You couldn't see it from there."

By now the Reds and Giants had seen their chance. "Don't get *mad*, Danny," they began to chant again.

Coach Wilkens called time-out and walked out to Danny. Kenny and Jenny walked over too.

Harlan knew exactly what the coach was saying: "It might have been a bad call, but that's part of baseball. Forget about it. Settle down. Get 'em out."

Danny was nodding. But the chanting was still going on.

The coach started back to his box, but he said to the umpire, "Son, that's not cheering going on up there. That kind of negative stuff isn't supposed to be allowed."

The young umpire looked around, but he did nothing. Harlan figured he didn't know what to do.

And when the ninth batter struck out—without so much as a decent swing—some of the noise in the bleachers died out.

The Dodgers would have been in good shape if the A's shortstop, a girl named McConnell, hadn't hit the ball right at Danny.

It was a line drive that should have stuck.

But it hit the heel of Danny's glove and dropped at his feet.

Danny didn't know where it had gone for a second. And then when he grabbed it, he still had an easy throw to get the runner at second.

But Danny threw right past Bunson, who was covering second. The ball rolled into left field.

The runners ended up on second and third.

And the chant had begun again.

"Don't get *mad*, Danny."

*"Don't get mad, Danny."*

But he *was* mad. He slammed his glove on the ground and then kicked it.

That was all it took.

Coach Wilkens called him off the field. And he sent Lian out to play second base.

Harlan took a deep breath. He hoped this would work out okay.

Danny walked to the dugout and kicked the bench. The Reds and Dodgers were yelling all kinds of stuff about the "baby boy" who was now playing second.

But Lian was smiling.

"He must not understand what all those guys are yelling," Jacob said.

"I think he knows exactly what's going on," Harlan said. "He just knows he's going to shut them up when he makes a big play. Look how confident he is."

"Maybe," Jacob said. "I hope that's what it is."

But Lian didn't get a chance to show anything to the next batter.

Kenny was throwing some serious heat.

The left fielder was up, and he was a solid hitter, but Kenny put a couple of pitches on the outside edge of the plate at the knees.

Perfect pitches.

Two strikes.

And then the batter struck out on a pitch on his fists.

"That's what I call pitching," Harlan said.

He watched Lian. The kid was still smiling, still waiting for his chance.

He didn't get it this time either.

But it wasn't Kenny who kept him from getting it.

Kenny got a strike on Bessant, the best hitter on the A's team, and then he tried to throw a curve. It never quite broke. It hung in the strike zone.

Bessant *murdered* the ball.

It would have been a homer if it had been up in the air. As it was, it hit the fence in left-center on one screaming bounce. Bessant had to stop at second, but both runs scored.

The A's dugout—and their fans—made plenty of noise. But the Giants and the Reds made a lot more.

"Keep it going, A's," Gerstein, the Reds' mouthy third baseman, was yelling at the top of his lungs. "The Dodgers don't have it anymore."

And then the next batter slapped a hot shot to the right side. It was headed for right field. Bessant would score.

But Lian had darted to his left, quick as a desert lizard, and he dove for the ball. Harlan was not sure Lian had it until he bounced to his feet, dug the ball from his glove, and hurled it—right on target—to Jenny for the putout.

*Wow!*

The crowd let out a gasp. They had just seen a major-league play by a kid who looked too little to play Little League.

"Did you see that?" people were saying.

Harlan spun around to look at the Reds. Winter, the Reds' catcher, was shaking his head. He didn't look happy.

Lian still had that same little smile on his face as he ran off the field. He didn't seem all that excited—just pleased.

And he certainly didn't seem surprised.

All the Dodgers were pounding on his back and yelling, "Great play, Lian. Great play."

"Thank you. Thank you," he kept saying.

And Bunson gave him a big slap too. "Hey, Line Drive, you can play," he said.

"Thank you."

Bunson was grinning. "Not bad," he said. He looked over at Harlan and seemed to see that I-told-you-so look on his face. "He might be really good when he gets bigger. I just wish he could hit the way Jeff did."

Harlan had to grant that much. They probably were giving up something there. But at least Lian could play the game.

"All right, let's get some runs," Coach Wilkens was yelling.

Harlan knew they still had a long way to go to win the game. Their lead was down to two runs.

# ★ **8** ★

# **In the Clutch**

But things didn't get any easier.

The A's were a much better team than they once were, and they had a lot of fans on their side.

The Angel Park supporters were out in full force, too, but they didn't seem as intense. Maybe they just expected the Dodgers to beat the A's.

The A's pitcher settled down. He didn't throw hard, but he had control, and he moved the ball around.

In the bottom of the third, Lian came up to bat with two out and nobody on base.

The Reds and Giants yelled all sorts of smart stuff.

"Scrunch down a little, kid. Your shoulders and knees will come together, and you won't have a strike zone."

"That bat is too big. Give the kid a toothpick."

But Lian didn't seem to care. He took two pitches high. Each time, he shook his head. Harlan could tell he wanted something in the strike zone.

The next pitch was also high, but Lian went after it. He fouled it off.

"He doesn't want to walk," Jacob said. "But he should. He could walk almost every time."

But Lian swung at another pitch, up in his eyes. This time he missed.

"What's the little goofus doing?" Bunson said.

"Hey," Coach Wilkens yelled at Bunson. "You let *me* talk to him about that. And don't you be calling him names."

But Lian swung again—at ball five?—and

popped the pitch up for the third out. Bunson mumbled something to Danny, but he kept his voice low.

The coach put Harlan and Jacob in the game at that point—Harlan at first and Jacob in right field.

Neither team scored in the fourth, and the pitchers seemed in control.

But then Kenny made a big mistake in the fifth inning. He was maybe a little too careful with McConnell, and he walked her.

Then, after getting the second out, he faced Bessant again.

Kenny got behind in the count and aimed a pitch down the middle. This time Bessant committed murder number two—except that he got the ball higher this time.

"In the *stratosphere*," Harlan whispered to himself, as the ball arched practically off the planet.

And now the game was tied.

Kenny was upset with himself.

But he got the side out without any more

damage, and the Dodgers had the heart of the batting order—Malone, Sandoval, and Bunson—coming up in the bottom of the fifth.

"Come on," Coach Wilkens yelled. He clapped his hands. "Let's get the momentum back. Good swings. Base hits."

But it didn't start out that way.

Malone hit a fly ball to left, and Kenny trickled a ball to the first baseman.

Bunson came up, stomping, chopping with his bat, ready to show Bessant what a *real* hit was like.

The Giants' and Reds' players were staying for the whole game. They were going nuts. They loved to see Bunson fail—but they also knew what he could do.

And this time he *crunched* one.

For a moment Harlan thought the ball was headed out of town. But Bunson had gotten under it a little too much.

It was a long fly—to the fence. But the left fielder waited, leaned against the fence . . .

Stretched up . . .

And caught it.

The game was going to the sixth inning, and the score was still 4 to 4.

Lian hadn't had another ball hit to him since his big play in the third inning. But the first two batters in the sixth hit grounders to his side.

Lian made the plays look easy. He was smooth and sure as he tossed the ball to Harlan, and the ball hit the glove as though it were a bull's-eye.

Harlan knew for sure now. Lian's problem that first day really had been with the uniform.

Now, if only his name really were Line Drive. If only he could hit the way he fielded. But that would only come with time—as he got bigger. Lots of great infielders in the major leagues were not really that tough with the bat.

Lian would be the third batter in the bottom of the inning. He was going to come up to bat with the pressure on. Harlan wondered whether the coach would put Danny back in.

But for right now Harlan had to worry about something even more important: *he* was up first.

And maybe Harlan lucked out a little. The A's coach yelled out to Sullivan, the pitcher, "Their worst hitters are coming up. No walks. Let's not get back around to the top of the order."

Maybe that made Harlan a little mad. But mostly it made the pitcher a little too set on throwing strikes and a little too relaxed about Harlan.

The first pitch was fat as a beach ball, and Harlan slugged it into center field.

Eddie didn't do quite so well. He hit the ball on the ground to the right side. Harlan moved to second on the play, but Eddie was out.

Someone needed to drive Harlan in, but the little guys were coming up: Lian and Brian Waters.

Lian was heading for the batter's box when Coach Wilkens called him back.

Harlan figured the coach must have decided to put Danny back in. But the coach was talking to Lian, not sending him to the dugout.

Harlan saw him motion with his hand over Lian's head, and he knew what he must be saying: "Don't swing at those high pitches."

Maybe the coach thought Lian could get a walk. But what good would that do? That would add a runner, but it would give the A's a force at second or third. The only thing that counted was getting Harlan home with the winning run.

Did the coach really think little Lian could get a hit?

Lian nodded, bowed, and walked to the plate.

The noise in the crowd suddenly increased ten times. The A's and the Giants and the Reds were all yelling the same kind of stuff:

"Whose little brother are you, kid?"

"Don't hurt yourself trying to swing that bat!"

The first pitch was high. Lian started to swing and held up. Then he looked down to the coach. His smile was back.

Again the pitch was high.

"Come on," the A's coach yelled. "This little kid can't hurt you. Get the ball in the strike zone."

And that's when the pitcher brought one down.

Little Lian lashed at the ball like an unwinding spring.

And *connected.*

The ball shot off his bat and into the gap between left and center field.

For a moment the whole place was silent, as though no one could believe it.

And then Bunson screamed at the top of his lungs, *"Line Drive!"*

Harlan never did know whether Bunson was yelling Lian's nickname or describing the hit. But Harlan knew *he* was rounding third and trotting on home—with the winning run!

And the whole Dodger team was running right past him, out to grab Lian. That was okay—Lian deserved it.

And Lian never changed his smile.

But he looked very satisfied when he got a ride on Bunson's and Sterling Malone's shoulders.

Harlan found time somewhere in the middle of all the confusion to look at the bleachers and see Winter and Gerstein, and all the Reds—plus all the Giants—just standing there looking shocked.

Winter's mouth was still hanging open.

Jeff was up there, too, standing on one foot, hopping and yelling and waving.

The team hadn't let him down this time!

But that was only the beginning of the good news. After the Dodgers slapped hands with the A's and celebrated a little with the coach, they all went up to watch the Reds and the Giants play each other.

And the Reds won!

Now the Giants had two losses, and the Reds and the Dodgers each had three. With two games left in the season, the Dodgers still had a chance for the second-half championship.

The rookies walked home together that Saturday, but they had a new friend with them. A line-drive hitter.

And all the way home, they gave him English lessons. They pointed to everything in sight and got him to say the word. Or sometimes he pointed and said, "Whassat?"

They told him. They told him everything. And then they went back to the park that afternoon and pointed out every part of a baseball field and taught him all those words.

"First base. Second base. Third base."

He got all those—and pronounced them pretty well.

And then he pointed to Harlan. "Good hitter," he said.

"Well, yeah, he got that right," Harlan said. And Kenny and Jacob laughed.

"I hit line drives. Nothing but line drives."
Harlan made the motion, to show what the
words meant.

"Line drive," Lian said, as best he could.

"Hey, you can hit 'em. You'll learn to say
it," Harlan said. "You learn fast."

Lian Jie kept smiling, still looking very
pleased.

And finally he told them why. "Friends,"
he said. "You are my friends."

# BOX SCORE, GAME 18

## Paseo A's 4

| | ab | r | h | rbi |
|---|---|---|---|---|
| McConnell ss | 1 | 2 | 0 | 0 |
| Chavez lf | 3 | 0 | 0 | 0 |
| Bessant 3b | 3 | 1 | 2 | 4 |
| Sullivan p | 3 | 0 | 0 | 0 |
| Santos 1b | 1 | 0 | 1 | 0 |
| Smith c | 3 | 0 | 0 | 0 |
| Watrous cf | 1 | 0 | 0 | 0 |
| Oshima 2b | 0 | 1 | 0 | 0 |
| Trout rf | 2 | 0 | 0 | 0 |
| Boston 2b | 1 | 0 | 0 | 0 |
| Powell 1b | 2 | 0 | 0 | 0 |
| De Klein cf | 2 | 0 | 1 | 0 |
| ttl | 22 | 4 | 4 | 4 |

## Angel Park Dodgers 5

| | ab | r | h | rbi |
|---|---|---|---|---|
| White 3b | 3 | 1 | 1 | 0 |
| Malone cf | 3 | 1 | 2 | 1 |
| Sandoval p | 3 | 1 | 1 | 1 |
| Bunson ss | 2 | 1 | 0 | 0 |
| Roper 1b | 2 | 0 | 1 | 1 |
| Boschi lf | 3 | 0 | 0 | 0 |
| Sandia 2b | 1 | 0 | 0 | 0 |
| Waters rf | 1 | 0 | 1 | 1 |
| Bacon c | 2 | 0 | 0 | 0 |
| Jie 2b | 2 | 0 | 1 | 1 |
| Scott rf | 1 | 0 | 0 | 0 |
| Sloan 1b | 1 | 1 | 1 | 0 |
| | 24 | 5 | 8 | 5 |

| | | | | | | |
|---|---|---|---|---|---|---|
| **A's** | 0 0 2 | 0 2 0—4 |
| **Dodgers** | 4 0 0 | 0 0 1—5 |

## League Standings After Eight Games:
## (Second Half of Season)

| | |
|---|---|
| Giants | 6–2 |
| Dodgers | 5–3 |
| Reds | 5–3 |
| Mariners | 4–4 |
| A's | 2–6 |
| Padres | 2–6 |

## Seventh-game scores:

| | | | |
|---|---|---|---|
| Giants | 3 | Dodgers | 0 |
| Mariners | 9 | Reds | 8 |
| A's | 4 | Padres | 3 |

## Eighth-game scores:

| | | | |
|---|---|---|---|
| Dodgers | 5 | A's | 4 |
| Reds | 9 | Giants | 7 |
| Padres | 15 | Mariners | 12 |

DEAN HUGHES has written many books for children including the popular *Nutty* stories and *Jelly's Circus*. He has also published such works of literary fiction for young adults as the highly acclaimed *Family Pose*. When he's not attending Little League games, Mr. Hughes devotes his full time to writing. He lives in Utah with his wife and family.

# ENTER THE ANGEL PARK ALL-STARS SWEEPSTAKES!

- The Grand Prize: a trip for four to the 1991 All-Star Game in Toronto
- 25 First Prizes: Louisville Slugger Little League bat personalized with the winner's name and the Angel Park All-Stars logo

## See official entry rules below.

### OFFICIAL RULES—NO PURCHASE NECESSARY

1. On an official entry form print your name, address, zip code, age, and the answer to the following question: What are the names of the three main characters in the Angel Park All-Stars books? The information needed to answer this question can be found in any of the Angel Park All-Stars books, or you may obtain an entry form, a set of rules, and the answer to the question by writing to: Angel Park Request, P.O. Box 3352, Syosset, NY 11775–3352. Each request must be mailed separately and must be received by November 1, 1990.

2. Enter as often as you wish, but each entry must be mailed separately to: ANGEL PARK ALL-STARS SWEEPSTAKES, P.O. Box 3335, Syosset, NY 11775–3335. No mechanically reproduced entries will be accepted. All entries must be received by December 1, 1990.

3. **Winners will be selected, from among correct entries received, in a random drawing conducted by National Judging Institute, Inc., an independent judging organization whose decisions are final on all matters relating to this sweepstakes. All prizes will be awarded and winners notified by mail. Prizes are nontransferable, and no substitutions or cash equivalents are allowed. Taxes, if any, are the responsibility of the individual winners. Winners may be asked to verify address or execute an affidavit of eligibility and release. No responsibility is assumed for lost, misdirected, or late entries or mail. Grand Prize consists of a three-day/two-night trip for a family of four to the 1991 All-Star Game in Toronto, Canada, including round-trip air transportation, hotel accommodations, game tickets, hotel-to-airport and hotel-to-game transfers, and breakfasts and dinners. In the event the trip is won by a minor, it will be awarded in the name of a parent or legal guardian. Trip must be taken on date specified or the prize will be forfeited and an alternate winner selected. RANDOM HOUSE, INC., and its affiliates reserve the right to use the prize winners' names and likenesses in any promotional activities relating to this sweepstakes without further compensation to the winners.**

4. Sweepstakes open to residents of the U.S. and Canada, except for the Province of Quebec. Employees and their families of RANDOM HOUSE, INC., and its affiliates, subsidiaries, advertising agencies, and retailers, and Don Jagoda Associates, Inc., may not enter. This offer is void wherever prohibited, and subject to all federal, state, and local laws.

5. **For a list of winners, send a stamped, self-addressed envelope to: ANGEL PARK WINNERS, P.O. Box 3347, Syosset, NY 11775–3347.**

..................................................................................................

## Angel Park All-Stars Sweepstakes Official Entry Form

Name:_____ Age:_____
(Please Print)

Address_____

City/State/Zip:_____


What are the names of the three main characters in the Angel Park All-Stars books?

_____